WORLD ECONOMY

What's the Future?

Matt Anniss

W
FRANKLIN WATTS
LONDON · SYDNEY

First published 2015 by Franklin Watts
338 Euston Road
London NW1 3BH

Franklin Watts Australia
Level 17/207 Kent Street
Sydney, NSW 2000

Produced by Calcium

A CIP catalogue record for this book is available from
the British Library.

ISBN 978 1 4451 3874 9

Dewey classification: 337

Printed in China

Franklin Watts is a division of Hachette Children's Books,
an Hachette UK company
www.hachette.co.uk

Acknowledgements:
The publisher would like to thank the following for permission to
reproduce photographs: Dreamstime: 1000words 12, Blacjack 15,
Dublinuser 14, Jborzicchi 21, Joaobambu 23, Kpikoulas 38, Paura 22,
Pinkcandy 32, Robcorbett cover (c), 35, Seast 20, Springdt313 19, Szirtesi
33, Tdmartin 29, Vacclav 34; Istockphoto: Mario Tama 5; Shutterstock:
Arindambanerjee 17, Chameleons Eye 28, Chaoss 41, Creative Images
24, P Cruciatti 18, 44, Ioana Davies 26, Fatseyeva 1, 16, Vlad Georgescu
11, Gil C 39, Goodluz 40, Bianda Ahmad Hisham cover (b), Michael Jung
10, Sergej Khakimullin cover (t), Kuzma 7, Daryl Lang 27, Rafael Ramirez
Lee 37, Frederic Legrand 30, Lisa S. 45, Losevsky Photo and Video 25,
Tan Wei Ming 4, Monkey Business Images 8, Paintings 43, Portokalis 13,
Michael Puche 31, Vasily Smirnov 36, Albert H. Teich 9, Tupungato 42.

Every attempt has been made to clear copyright. Should there be any
inadvertent omission please apply to the publisher for rectification.

Contents

If you open up a newspaper or turn on a television news channel, you often find headlines about money matters around the world. The world economy has been through a turbulent time in recent years, and is only just recovering from a deep recession. What is the economy, and why is it so often in the media?

An uncertain future

The economy is what experts call the system by which money is created, exchanged and moved around a country and, in turn, around the world. When times are good, companies are productive, and people are more likely to buy and sell things. This creates more jobs and more money, so a country's gross domestic product (the total value of goods and services produced in one year) is high.

FACE FACTS

'As sure as the spring will follow the winter, prosperity and economic growth will follow recession.'
Bo Bennett,
Internet millionaire

Some countries, such as China, have enjoyed a booming economy while others were in recession.

10 DEC 2019

The world economy was thrown into turmoil after the failure of the banking system in 2008.

GOING DOWN

When an economy is in bad shape, there is less money in the system, fewer jobs and people spend less. When an economy has been weak for at least six months, it is said to be in recession. According to most experts, the world economy suffered a very bad recession in 2008, from which many countries are only now beginning to recover.

EXPERT OPINION

In this book, we will look in detail at the future of the world economy, asking whether things are going to get better or worse in the years ahead. We will also look at the way some economies around the world are booming, while others are struggling.

ask the experts

MOST EXPERTS AGREE THAT THE RECENT ECONOMIC CRISIS IS THE WORST SINCE THE GREAT DEPRESSION IN THE 1930s, WHEN MILLIONS OF PEOPLE LOST THEIR JOBS AND HOMES. THERE HAS BEEN MUCH DISAGREEMENT OVER THE EFFECTS OF THE RECESSION, HOWEVER. SOME SAY THAT CERTAIN ECONOMIES MAY NEVER FULLY RECOVER, WHILE OTHERS THINK THEY ARE NOW BOUNCING BACK. WHO IS RIGHT?

Recession is not a new thing. Throughout history, the fortunes of countries have risen and fallen in line with their economies. Experts call this 'boom and bust'. In recent years, many countries have experienced recession. So how did this happen?

Crash and burn

During the 1990s and early 2000s, many countries enjoyed a 'boom' period. Credit, which means people can borrow money and pay it back later, was more available than ever before. People did not worry about paying off their loans – living with debt became a way of life.

After 2008, protests about the poor state of the economy became news headlines in the West.

BANKER ATE ALL THE PIES

FACE FACTS

'The world has been spending staggering amounts of money that it does not have for a few decades now, and it is all coming home to roost.'
Jim Rogers, international investment banker

When the economy crashes, some people lose their homes and are forced to sleep on the streets.

ALL FALL DOWN

In the autumn of 2007, our money systems started to unravel. In the United States, a number of banks began to lose money quickly, as it became clear that they had lent money to people who could not pay them back. Within a year, the crisis had spread worldwide. Very quickly, governments had to step in to save the banks from running out of money.

DOWNTURN

Things quickly went from bad to worse. People lost their jobs and with it their homes, which they bought with loans from banks that were close to collapse. As a result, most people found that they had a lot less money, and many people did not have any spare money for luxuries, entertainment or holidays.

NO WAY BACK?

The health of the world economy is based on people creating, earning and spending money. Until people have more money, they cannot spend it. However, until people spend more money, the economy cannot recover. Governments need to find ways to create more jobs and make people wealthier so they start buying again.

Gambling with our future

Many experts say that the recent recession can be blamed on the banks. They say that the banks did not carry out enough checks before they lent money to companies, governments and individuals. When people and organisations could not pay back the money they owed, the banks became short of money and the economy failed.

Easy come, easy go

In the years leading up to the economic crash in 2008, many banks in the United States and Europe lent money to people so that they could buy their own homes. The banks made money by charging people interest to borrow money from them. However, many of these people could not afford to repay their loans, but the banks still lent them the money. These loans became bad debts. When the banks realised they were unlikely to get their money back, many sold on the debts to other banks around the world. The problem then got bigger as more and more banks owned bad debts, which became known as 'toxic debts'.

FACE FACTS

'Time is running out fast. I think we maybe have a few months – it could be weeks, it could be days – before financial catastrophe.' Willem Buiter, chief economist, Citigroup, November, 2011

When it became clear that the banks were in trouble, stockbrokers lost confidence in the economy and panic set in worldwide.

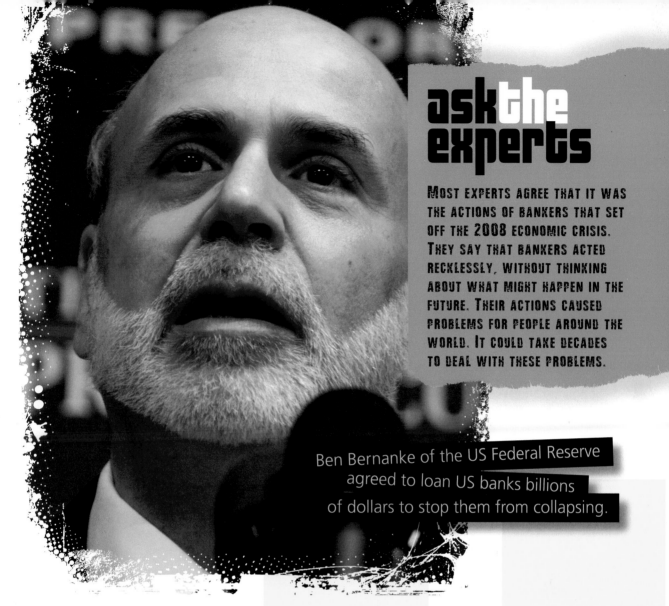

MOST EXPERTS AGREE THAT IT WAS THE ACTIONS OF BANKERS THAT SET OFF THE 2008 ECONOMIC CRISIS. THEY SAY THAT BANKERS ACTED RECKLESSLY, WITHOUT THINKING ABOUT WHAT MIGHT HAPPEN IN THE FUTURE. THEIR ACTIONS CAUSED PROBLEMS FOR PEOPLE AROUND THE WORLD. IT COULD TAKE DECADES TO DEAL WITH THESE PROBLEMS.

Ben Bernanke of the US Federal Reserve agreed to loan US banks billions of dollars to stop them from collapsing.

HOUSE OF CARDS

In 2008, it was the collapse of a large international bank called Lehman Brothers that set off the world economic crisis. Many smaller banks around the world were dependent on Lehman Brothers. Once the large bank closed, the smaller banks ran out of money. Others were saved from the brink of closure by money from national governments. In order to hold onto the money they did have, banks stopped lending money to businesses and individuals, even to those who could afford to pay it back. A healthy economy needs banks to lend to people, so they can grow their businesses. Without lending, money stops passing through the system and the economy falls into recession.

CASINO BANKING

Since the 2008 crisis, many banks have recovered and are making money again. Experts say that the banks recklessly gambled with our money – they may have recovered, but many economies are recovering far more slowly.

9

Many people have used credit cards to buy goods, leading to big debts that they cannot afford to repay.

THE DEBT CRISIS

The biggest single problem currently affecting the world economy is debt. Individuals, companies and governments around the world have many debts. The level of debt has been rising for decades. Many experts think that it was a reliance on borrowing too much money that caused the economy to crash in 2008. The question now is how can we repay the huge sums of money that we owe?

askthe experts

EXPERTS AGREE THAT SOVEREIGN DEBT IS ONE OF THE GREATEST PROBLEMS FACING THE WORLD RIGHT NOW. SOVEREIGN DEBT IS THE TOTAL AMOUNT OF MONEY OWED BY EACH COUNTRY. EXPERTS SAY THAT IF WE DO NOT CREATE WAYS TO BOOST THE ECONOMY, MANY COUNTRIES COULD RUN OUT OF MONEY IN THE NEXT 20 YEARS. IF THIS HAPPENS, ANOTHER SEVERE WORLD CRISIS WOULD OCCUR.

GOVERNMENT BORROWING

Many governments around the world are deeply in debt. This is because they have borrowed money to pay for public services, such as building schools or hospitals, or to buy weapons for wars. Whatever the reason, many nations now owe vast sums that they may struggle to pay back in the future.

The amount of money owed by nations is truly staggering. The United States is estimated to have around $17 trillion (£10 trillion) worth of debt, according to current statistics, while the United Kingdom owes more than £1.27 trillion. The total amount of 'sovereign debt' worldwide is rising year on year.

TROUBLE AHEAD?

When times are good and there is a lot of money in the economy, sovereign debt is not a problem because governments can easily meet the payments they must make on these loans. However, when times are bad, it can become an enormous problem.

To pay their debts, governments must either spend less money by cutting public services, or raise more money by increasing the taxes people pay. These policies make it harder for the country's economy to grow. The policies are also unpopular with ordinary people, who are taxed to raise money and who lose out when public services are cut.

FACE FACTS

'Today we spend more on paying back debts than we do on running schools. For every single pound Britons pay in tax, 10 pence is spent on debt repayment.'
David Cameron,
British Prime Minister

The large amount of money borrowed by the UK government in recent years has led to a sizeable sovereign debt.

TROUBLE BREWING

When the world economy crashes, it is not just a lack of money in the system we have to worry about. Often, the issues caused by a broken economy – a lack of jobs, mass poverty and people losing their homes – can trigger huge problems in society such as crime, riots and even the fall of governments.

PEACEFUL PROTESTS

When people see themselves becoming poorer as a result of a failing economy, it makes them angry. Sometimes people express their anger through peaceful protests, such as marches or demonstrations. In 2011 and 2012, the 'Occupy' movement around the world was an example of this anger. People set up camps in high-profile locations to express their views and outrage.

The way in which the UK government handled the recent crisis in the economy led to protests in London.

FACE FACTS

'The choice we face is one of sacrifice or even greater sacrifice – on a scale that cannot be compared.'
Evangelos Venizelos, Finance Minister, Greece

Violence on the streets

If a government is forced to make extreme cuts, it increases the likelihood that angry and frustrated people will turn to violence. Since 2010, Greece has been torn apart by rioting on the streets resulting from the country's huge economic problems. The Greek government had to ask other European nations to lend Greece more than £65 billion, to prevent the country's economy from falling apart.

Austerity measures

To obtain the money, the Greek government had to agree to introduce severe 'austerity measures' in their country. This meant that the Greek government had to spend less on services but still had to raise even more taxes to pay off its huge debts.

Greece has seen both peaceful and violent protests against government action taken to deal with its financial crisis.

ask the experts

Many experts say that what has happened in Greece is a warning to other nations in trouble. They say that there is a strong chance that trouble like this could occur in other parts of the world where the economy is weak and unstable. However, most agree that unpopular austerity measures are essential to solve the economic problems in countries such as Greece.

Anger turns to protest

The austerity policies were extremely unpopular, because they made most people much poorer. Many people in Greece felt their government was responsible for getting them into such enormous debt. The people felt they were suffering because of the mistakes of both the bankers and the government. Soon, some people's rage turned to angry protests on the streets.

13

THE COMEBACK KIDS

Over the last 15 years, a number of countries have run out of money to pay off their many debts and have been declared 'bankrupt'. This means they were unable to pay their debt. Now, many of these countries are booming, with strong economies. They are the world economy's 'comeback kids'.

GOING BUST

In 2001, Argentina was engulfed in a massive crisis when its economy collapsed. Members of the public, worried about losing their savings, lined up all night outside banks to withdraw their money. Faced with debts of more than £85 billion, Argentina's president was forced to announce to the world that his country had gone bust.

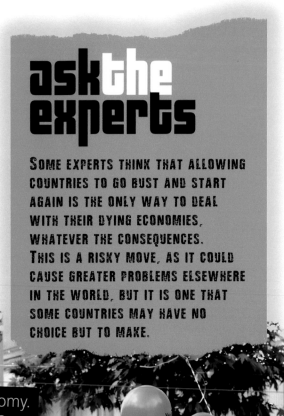

ask the experts

SOME EXPERTS THINK THAT ALLOWING COUNTRIES TO GO BUST AND START AGAIN IS THE ONLY WAY TO DEAL WITH THEIR DYING ECONOMIES, WHATEVER THE CONSEQUENCES. THIS IS A RISKY MOVE, AS IT COULD CAUSE GREATER PROBLEMS ELSEWHERE IN THE WORLD, BUT IT IS ONE THAT SOME COUNTRIES MAY HAVE NO CHOICE BUT TO MAKE.

Ireland has taken steps to boost its economy. Its business taxes are at a record low to attract investors such as Google.

The German chancellor Angela Merkel has led EU talks to try to stop failing European economies from going bust.

GROWING ECONOMY

In 2002, in Argentina a new government was elected. They put money into public services to make sure that people could survive the crisis. They also cut taxes and encouraged businesses to grow. Soon, countries around the world were buying more Argentine products, such as soy and beef, and the economy quickly recovered. Today, Argentina is thriving and has one of the fastest-growing economies in the world.

FIGHTING BACK

In 2008, Iceland suffered similar problems to Argentina. Yet between 2010 and 2012, the country's economy grew rapidly. A similar thing is now happening to Ireland, a country that just escaped going bust in 2008. The government lowered taxes to attract outside investment from businesses such as Google, and the economy is bouncing back as a result.

FACE FACTS

'The best way to avoid a bust is to avoid having an unsustainable boom in the first place. Unfortunately, that is a lesson that none of us seems to learn.'
Matthew Partridge, business journalist

The 2008 recession did not affect all parts of the world. While countries with traditionally strong economies such as the United States, the United Kingdom, France and Spain were hit by recession, other nations saw their fortunes rise. Countries whose economies were not closely linked to the banking system were able to ride out the storm and emerge stronger.

A new world order

The United Arab Emirates is an oil-rich country that has not been affected by the global economic crisis.

FACE FACTS

'It is realistic to say that within 10 years, China's economy will be roughly the same size as the US economy.'
Tom Miller, economist, GK Dragonomics, 2011

Many computer firms have opened up factories in China and India, where it is cheaper to make products.

Developing powers

Many of the world's fastest-growing economies are in Asia, the Middle East and South America. These are places that, until recently, did not have the systems or structures in place to compete with the United States and Europe. Now they do, and they want to use this advantage to transform themselves into economic superpowers.

Changing times

Experts think that this could be the first stage of a 'new world order', with new economic superpowers leading the world forwards. Soon, it may be China, India, Saudi Arabia and Brazil calling the shots, not the United States and Europe. It may take a while, but the developing world may one day dominate the world economy.

ask the experts

EXPERTS AGREE THAT ALTHOUGH THERE ARE MANY COUNTRIES WITH THE POTENTIAL TO BECOME NEW 'ECONOMIC SUPERPOWERS', THIS WILL NOT HAPPEN OVERNIGHT. THEY SAY THAT IT WILL TAKE AT LEAST A DECADE FOR CHINA TO OVERTAKE THE UNITED STATES AS THE WORLD'S BIGGEST ECONOMY, AND MANY MORE FOR INDIA AND OTHER DEVELOPING NATIONS TO COMPETE.

Unstoppable China?

The economies of Asian countries are set to grow by 6.9 per cent each year between 2014 and 2018, which is a sizeable economic growth rate. Helping to fuel this growth is China. In 2013 alone, the Chinese economy grew by 7.7 per cent. This meant that the country was hundreds of billions of pounds richer than it was the year before. Most experts say that China will overtake the United States as the world's biggest single economy by 2020. One expert, Anvind Subramanian, says the country already has, and that the change took place in 2010. Whoever you believe, China is fast becoming the world's number one economic force.

"THE DEBATE

Can China's economy keep growing as fast as it has in recent years? Some experts think that over the next 30 years, China's economy will stop growing as other nations catch up. Others say that the opposite will happen, and it will continue to grow as demand for products increases worldwide. "

Today, China has a thriving economy that threatens to topple the great economic superpowers in the West.

Chinese workers are skilled at making electrical products such as mobile phones, iPads and laptop computers.

FACE FACTS

'China was top dog economically for thousands of years. In some ways, the past few hundred years have just been a blip.'
Anvind Subramanian, economist and writer

THE WORLD'S FACTORY

It costs less to make things in China than in the United States or Europe. This is mostly because workers' wages are lower in China. Because of this, many companies are setting up factories in the country. Now, everything from iPods and computers to clothes and trainers are made in China. In 2011, more than £108 billion worth of products were exported from China to be sold overseas.

CHEAP LABOUR

Another factor in China's rise is the number of people who live in the country. It has a population of more than 1.2 billion. That is a lot of people who can work in factories, for lower wages, in order for people in the West to buy cheap mobile phones and televisions.

It is almost impossible for the United States and Europe to compete with China. Most people in the West demand much higher wages to do the same job that a worker in China will do for far less money. It costs the West more to produce goods, and most countries simply cannot compete with China.

The Indian boom

In many ways, the transformation of India from a developing country into a new economic superpower has been even more amazing than that of China. The country's economy is now six times bigger than it was 20 years ago. That is a remarkable turnaround. Some experts now think that the Indian economy is the third biggest in the world.

Low wages

Like China, India has profited from offering its services to the world. Also like China, products can be made very cheaply in India. This is because most Indian workers are paid much lower wages than their American or European counterparts. Another advantage the country has is that it can build factories in which to make goods very cheaply.

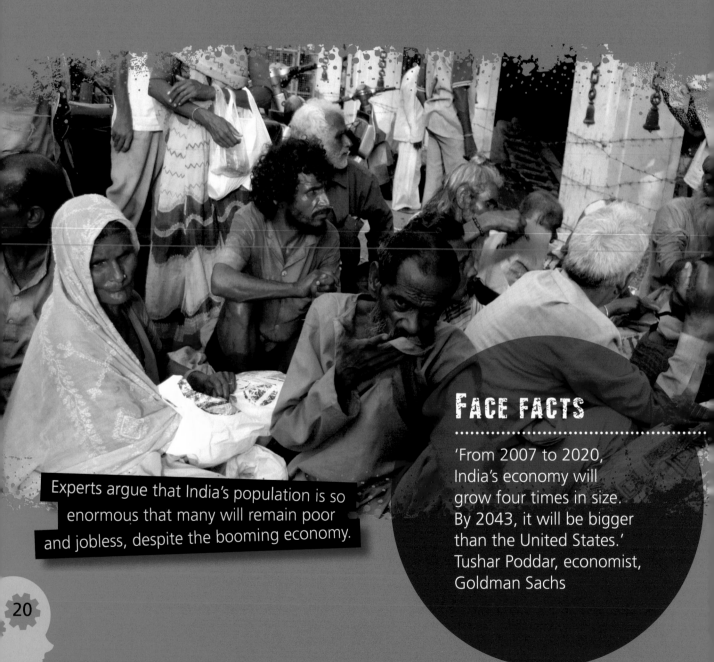

Experts argue that India's population is so enormous that many will remain poor and jobless, despite the booming economy.

FACE FACTS

'From 2007 to 2020, India's economy will grow four times in size. By 2043, it will be bigger than the United States.' Tushar Poddar, economist, Goldman Sachs

India's car industry is one of the fastest-growing in the world, thanks to the country's huge demand for vehicles.

Boom sectors

Although India still does not make as many products as China, some industries are booming. For example, many international drug companies now choose to make their pills and medicines in factories in the country. Another booming industry in India is clothing manufacturing. Currently, more than 20 per cent of the country's workforce is employed making clothes.

Call centres

Another rapid area of expansion in India has been the country's service industry. One of the official languages of India is English, and many English-speaking people are employed in telephone call centres. Many companies in the United Kingdom use call centres to offer customer services, such as advice and assistance, to their customers. It is cheaper to employ people in India to do this than it would be to employ British workers. The time difference also makes it easier for companies to offer their customers a 24-hour service.

ask the experts

MOST EXPERTS AGREE THAT INDIA'S ECONOMY WILL CONTINUE GROWING QUICKLY IN THE COMING YEARS. HOWEVER, MANY EXPERTS THINK THAT INDIA HAS TO SPEND MORE MONEY ON ITS INFRASTRUCTURE, INCLUDING ROADS, PORTS AND AIRPORTS, IF IT WANTS ITS BOOMING ECONOMY TO CONTINUE TO GROW AT THE SAME RATE.

The Brazilian boom

As the largest country in South America, Brazil has always been thought of as an economic superpower in waiting. Now, thanks to a huge boom in business in the last decade, Brazil has one of the fastest-growing economies in the world.

Carnival of business

Like other developing nations on the rise, Brazil's economy is getting bigger every year. It is now the sixth-largest economy in the world, and is predicted to be the fifth-largest by the middle of 2013. Brazil is a vast country, with a lot of natural resources such as farmland, oil and gas. This means it is in a very strong position to continue growing.

ask the experts

DESPITE HUGE GROWTH IN RECENT YEARS, EXPERTS SAY THAT BRAZIL'S ECONOMY MAY NOT BE AS STRONG AS PREVIOUSLY THOUGHT. ALTHOUGH MANY STILL BELIEVE THAT THE COUNTRY WILL BECOME THE WORLD'S FOURTH-BIGGEST ECONOMY BY 2050, SOME SAY STATISTICS SHOW THAT BRAZIL COULD FALL INTO RECESSION IN THE NEAR FUTURE.

It is hoped that Brazil's booming economy will mean that fewer of its people are forced to live in 'favelas', or shantytowns, such as this one.

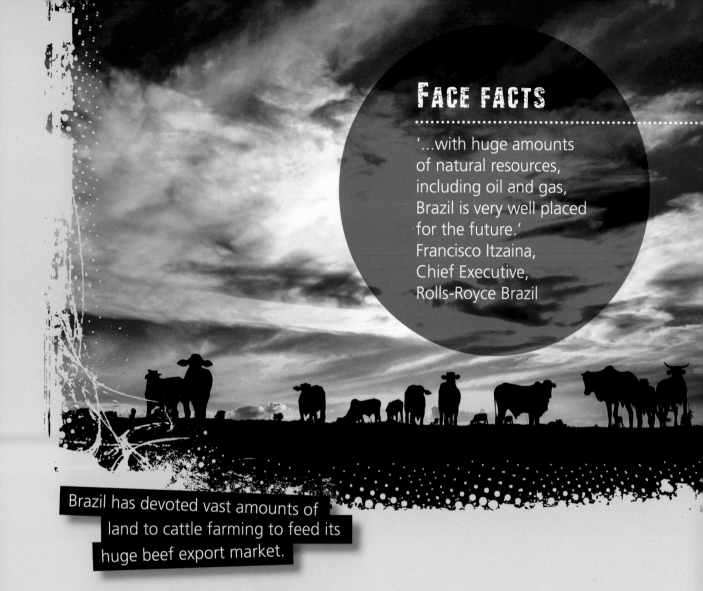

Brazil has devoted vast amounts of land to cattle farming to feed its huge beef export market.

AN EXPORT BOOM

Brazil's boom has been driven by an increase in exports, which are goods produced and sold to other countries. Brazil is the world's biggest producer of iron. It also exports more beef, chicken, orange juice, sugar, coffee and tobacco than any other nation on Earth. The country is also the home of the world's largest aircraft maker, Embraer.

CLEVER DEALS

Brazil has been clever in who it chooses to do business with. China is its biggest trade partner, and much of the food and drink that Brazil produces goes to Asia. As China is the largest nation on Earth, it is unlikely that orders to Brazil will dry up in the near future. If anything, Brazil will have to increase its production output to satisfy the levels of demand in its Asian markets.

New players

Although they are relatively small in size, a handful of countries in the Middle East are fast becoming some of the most important players on the global economic scene. Their extreme wealth, which is based on sales of oil and gas, is now being used to invest in building projects and to buy businesses around the world.

Oil riches

The Middle East produces more oil and gas than anywhere else on Earth. These are two of the most precious natural resources in the world. The business of extracting and selling these resources has made a handful of sheikhs, the traditional rulers of Arab countries, very rich indeed. As a result, their countries are also very wealthy.

Some wealthy Arab states have invested in spectacular building projects, such as this one in Abu Dhabi.

FACE FACTS

'Control over the production and distribution of oil is the decisive factor in defining who rules the Middle East.' Christopher Hitchens, journalist

Middle East nations such as the United Arab Emirates and Saudi Arabia have made their wealth through oil exports.

Small country, strong and growing economy

One of the most remarkable nations of the Middle East is the United Arab Emirates. The country is home to just 8 million people, but it has the 30th largest economy in the world. In recent years, the price of oil has increased as supplies have become much scarcer around the world. Because of this, the economy of the United Arab Emirates is growing in size year after year.

Wise spenders

The rulers of the United Arab Emirates have used the extra money in their economy wisely. As well as spending billions of pounds on building hotels in their two biggest cities, Dubai and Abu Dhabi, they have also set themselves up as an alternative to traditional banks. Over the last 10 years, they have lent money to other countries and invested almost £238 billion in many lucrative building projects around the world.

ask the experts

EXPERTS SAY THAT THE GROWTH OF MIDDLE EASTERN ECONOMIES COULD SLOW DOWN IN FUTURE YEARS UNLESS THEY CREATE MORE JOBS. ACCORDING TO A GROUP OF EXPERTS, ARAB COUNTRIES WILL NEED TO CREATE 75 MILLION EXTRA JOBS FOR YOUNG PEOPLE IN THE NEXT 10 YEARS, JUST TO KEEP PEOPLE EMPLOYED AND PREVENT POVERTY IN SECTIONS OF THE POPULATION.

The aftershocks of the 2008 banking crisis are still being felt around the world. While China, India and other fast-rising economic superpowers-in-waiting are forging ahead, many Western countries continue to struggle, weighed down by billions of pounds of debts. Is this the beginning of the end for these countries, or just another blip on the radar?

In the West

Wall Street in New York is the centre of the financial services industry in the United States. Will it be the centre of the world economy in the future?

ask the experts

MANY EXPERTS THINK THAT THE ECONOMIES OF THE WESTERN POWERS COULD TAKE UP TO 20 YEARS TO FULLY RECOVER FROM THE 2008 CRISIS. THEY POINT TO WHAT HAPPENED IN JAPAN IN THE 1990s, WHEN A 'LOST DECADE' FOLLOWED A SEVERE ECONOMIC CRASH. IF EXPERTS ARE RIGHT, MANY WESTERN COUNTRIES COULD EXPERIENCE A 'LOST DECADE' OF THEIR OWN.

The 'Occupy Wall Street' movement of 2011 was a protest against the Wall Street banking system, which some people believed had helped bring about the 2008 economic crisis.

EVER-CHANGING

The economy is a complicated system. It changes all the time as stock markets, in which money and shares in companies are bought and sold, rise and fall again. Economists have many conflicting ideas about how best to achieve a successful economy. At present, most simply do not agree on the best way forwards.

CONFLICTING IDEAS

Some economists think that the basis of a strong economy lies in making and selling goods to other countries. This is called exporting. Others think that the key to success lies in building strong banks and financial services. These sections of the economy are the businesses that buy and sell money and shares in companies.

CONFUSION

Right now, nobody knows what the future holds. In the past, the traditional Western powers, led by the United States, developed strong banking and financial services in their economies. When those industries collapsed in 2008, it brought many economies to the brink of destruction. So, where do we go next, and will our economies fully recover from the financial crisis?

27

FACE FACTS

'Economic growth without social progress lets the great majority of people remain in poverty, while a few reap the benefits.'
John F. Kennedy, US President 1961–63

A large number of Americans were made homeless during the 2008 economic crisis after losing their jobs.

THE UNITED STATES IN DECLINE?

The United States is the world's original economic superpower. Since the end of the British Empire in the mid-twentieth century, the United States has been the leader on the world stage. With China and India following close behind, the country now faces a fight to remain the world's largest economy.

IN RECESSION

Since the economic crash of 2008, the United States has felt the effects of a deep recession. Many companies have closed, leaving millions of people without jobs. In the summer of 2010, one in 10 American adults was out of work – that is about 10 per cent of the working population. This has since fallen to 8 per cent, but there are still more than 12 million unemployed Americans.

Easing answer?

President Obama has tried to end the US recession by pumping hundreds of billions of dollars into the economy in a process called 'quantitative easing'. The money was given to banks, so that they would lend it to businesses. The hope was that these businesses would create many new jobs. Unfortunately, so far this strategy has not worked.

Gloomy outlook

If the US economy's recovery continues to be slow, it may lose its position as the world's biggest economy. The government is trying to kick-start the economy, but it is proving very difficult to do. Experts warn that if the economy does not pick up soon, the country could slip into a permanent decline.

" THE DEBATE

Experts disagree about what the United States should be doing to address its problems. Some people think that the only way to get the economy going again is to cut taxes, so that people have more money in their pockets to spend on goods and services. Other experts disagree. They say that the way to fix the economy is to encourage businesses to create more jobs. If more people are working, they have money to spend on goods and services. Furthermore, if they are employed in making goods, the goods can be exported around the world. "

Since the 2008 banking crisis, President Obama has tried many strategies to try to help the economy.

A DEBT CRISIS?

One of the biggest problems faced by the Western countries are their levels of debt. The UK government currently owes around £1.27 trillion, and it is spending around £50 billion in interest owed on that sum each year. Is the government simply storing up problems for future generations?

David Cameron claims that overspending before the 2008 banking crisis has left the UK government heavily in debt.

INTEREST EXPLAINED

If you take a loan from a bank, you have to pay back the money over a certain period of time. An extra amount is added to the amount you originally borrowed. This is interest. The interest is a percentage of the total amount you borrow. The longer you take to pay off the loan, the more interest you have to pay. Since the UK government owes so much money, its yearly interest payments could be more than £75 billion by 2020.

ask the experts

EXPERTS AGREE THAT THE DEBTS OF THE UNITED KINGDOM ARE A BIG PROBLEM, BUT THEY DISAGREE ABOUT HOW TO DEAL WITH IT. SOME ECONOMISTS BELIEVE THAT THE GOVERNMENT SHOULD FOCUS ITS EFFORTS ON ADDRESSING THE PROBLEM. OTHERS BELIEVE THAT FOCUSING ONLY ON REDUCING THE DEBT WILL HARM THE UK'S FUTURE ECONOMY.

In the United Kingdom people have protested about how the government has handled the economy over the last few years.

Pay now, buy later

Many experts believe that the UK government should pay off more of its debt. To do this, the government would have to find much more money, either by raising taxes or by cutting the amount it spends. However, if it does this, it risks weakening the UK economy even more. If people have less money, they cannot boost the economy by buying things. The economy is a delicate balance.

An important time

The way the UK economy develops over the next few years could shape the country's future. If the economy continues to improve, the government will earn more in taxes and will pay off more of the debt. If it does not continue to improve, things could get worse for ordinary people, and the country's debts could pull it even further into trouble.

The end of the European dream?

The debt problems of the United Kingdom are serious, but some other countries inside the European Union (EU) have faced economic crises that have brought their countries to the point of collapse. There, many countries including Spain, Portugal, Italy and Greece, have teetered on the edge of disaster.

Eurozone problems

Seventeen countries in Europe share a currency, known as the euro. These are called the eurozone countries. Because all of these countries use the same currency, their financial problems are shared. That means that if the economy of just one of the eurozone countries collapses, its failure could put the whole eurozone at risk.

A worsening crisis

Many eurozone countries have struggled with high levels of national debt. When the recession caused by the 2008 banking crash deepened, some countries were unable to make their huge debt repayments.
To date, the European Central Bank, led by Germany, has had to 'bail out' Greece, Ireland and Portugal to stop their economies from collapsing. This means that the Central Bank has given these countries many billions of euros.

The nations within the eurozone have struggled to bring a huge economic crisis under control.

Face facts

'Germany remains the economic stronghold of the eurozone.'
Carsten Brzeski, economist, ING

BAD NEWS

Experts fear that the recent economic crisis within the eurozone has revealed a fundamental weakness within the EU. They say that the EU system is flawed because the economies of each country within it are not equal. Some countries, such as Germany, have strong economies and are 'propping up' the economies of much weaker countries, such as Greece. Experts say that unless all the economies within the Union are strong, bail outs could continue to be a feature of the system, which may ultimately lead to the collapse of the entire EU. Such an economic disaster would have a serious impact on the world economy.

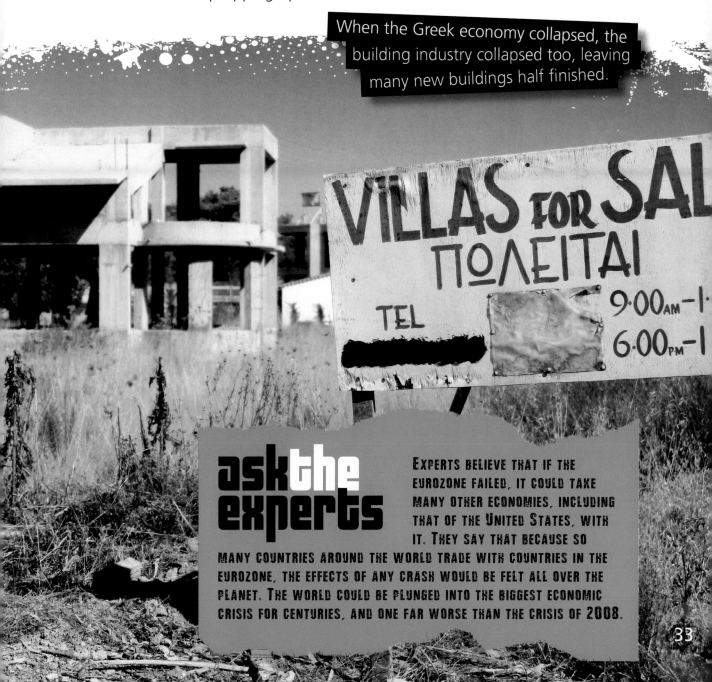

When the Greek economy collapsed, the building industry collapsed too, leaving many new buildings half finished.

VILLAS FOR SAL
ΠΟΛΕΙΤΑΙ
TEL
9·00ᴀᴍ–1·
6·00ᴘᴍ–1

askthe experts

EXPERTS BELIEVE THAT IF THE EUROZONE FAILED, IT COULD TAKE MANY OTHER ECONOMIES, INCLUDING THAT OF THE UNITED STATES, WITH IT. THEY SAY THAT BECAUSE SO MANY COUNTRIES AROUND THE WORLD TRADE WITH COUNTRIES IN THE EUROZONE, THE EFFECTS OF ANY CRASH WOULD BE FELT ALL OVER THE PLANET. THE WORLD COULD BE PLUNGED INTO THE BIGGEST ECONOMIC CRISIS FOR CENTURIES, AND ONE FAR WORSE THAN THE CRISIS OF 2008.

The lessons of history

Experts say that the recent recession may have been the worst the world has ever seen. However, it is by no means the first. Throughout the last 100 years, the world economy has been hit by many recessions and recovered. What can we learn from the economic disasters of the past?

Boom and bust

Most recessions happen after a period of quick economic growth. Eventually, the economy gets too big and the prices of shares in companies fall dramatically.

This triggers a collapse. One of the worst recessions ever seen was the Great Depression of the 1930s. It was triggered by the stock exchange crash on Wall Street in October 1929.

FACE FACTS

'My daughter asked me, "What is the economic crisis?" and I said, "It is something that happens every five to seven years."'
Jamie Dimon, Chief Executive, JP Morgan

This statue commemorates the victims of the Great Depression. Millions of people were made homeless and hungry by the 1930s' crisis.

ask the experts

MANY EXPERTS BELIEVE THAT RECESSIONS, HOWEVER PAINFUL, ARE AN INEVITABLE CONSEQUENCE OF THE WAY OUR ECONOMY WORKS. THEY SAY THAT ANY ECONOMY CANNOT CONTINUE GROWING FOREVER. AT SOME POINT IT WILL WEAKEN AND CRASH. THEY CALL THIS "BOOM AND BUST". WE ARE JUST EMERGING FROM A BUST PERIOD. IS OUR ECONOMY ABOUT TO BOOM AGAIN?

Some protesters fear that the effects of the recent recession could be longer-lasting than those of the Great Depression of the 1930s.

THE GREAT RECESSION

The Great Depression had a crippling effect on the United States, and many other countries around the world. At one point, one-quarter of all American adults were without work. All trade between countries was cut in half. Eventually, the world economy grew again, but it took many years for the system to fully recover from the crisis.

HISTORY REPEATING

The 1980s were another period of great economic growth around the world. That came to a shuddering halt in 1987, with another Wall Street crash. It was so bad that the leading companies in the United States lost almost one-quarter of their value. It took until the late 1990s for the world economy to fully recover.

35

Some experts believe that making more goods in the United Kingdom and selling them abroad is the quickest way to solve the UK's problems.

What does the future hold for the world economy? In banks and boardrooms all around the world, economists and other experts are asking themselves the same question. What are the economic challenges facing our leaders and our money experts over the next few years?

Into the future

Our most pressing problem is national debt. This problem could see the International Monetary Fund (IMF) and the World Bank play a bigger role in the world economy. These two organisations lend money to governments when they are in crisis. However, both of them are funded by payments from governments. If governments fail to pay back their loans, could even these banks eventually run out of money?

HACKING

There is another potential problem facing the world economy. When criminals attack international computer systems, it is called hacking. Today, most trade, business and banking is done using computers. Could computer hackers bring down the economy?

CANNOT AGREE

We also have to deal with the politics of the economic situation. Our politicians rarely agree on what is best for the economy, and it is the same around the world. The decisions politicians make now could affect the economy for many years to come. If the world economy continues to struggle, we could see an enormous rise in extreme governments. And their ideas about how to deal with the economic crisis will be radical.

A mass organised attack by computer hackers could rob banks of billions of pounds, leaving our accounts empty.

ask the experts

ECONOMISTS AGREE THAT WE ARE FACING A LONG PERIOD OF UNCERTAINTY, AS GRADUAL CHANGES IN THE WORLD ECONOMY TAKE PLACE. THEY ALL SAY THAT GOVERNMENTS IN THE UNITED STATES AND EUROPE MUST CONTINUE TO ADDRESS THEIR PROBLEMS. FAILURE TO ACT NOW COULD LEAD TO EVEN GREATER DISASTER IN THE FUTURE.

How deep are our pockets?

The global economy is supported by two organisations founded in 1944, towards the end of the Second World War. They are the IMF and the World Bank. These institutions exist to prevent global economic meltdown. In the years to come, they will play a huge role in the economic affairs of countries worldwide.

How the IMF works

The IMF gets its money directly from its members, namely the countries of the world. Each country must pay a certain amount to the IMF each year, depending on how wealthy it is.

The richest countries pay the most, and the poorest pay the least. The IMF holds the money in its central reserves, ready to use in the event of an economic crisis.

Face facts

'The world is governed by institutions that are not democratic: the World Bank, the IMF and the World Trade Organisation.'
Jose Sarrango,
Nobel Prize winner

Some protesters have accused the IMF of being undemocratic, and working to further the interests of the United States and Europe.

LENDING A HAND

If a country gets into trouble, it can apply to the IMF for a loan. Since 1991, the amount loaned by the IMF to countries in trouble has increased by one-fifth. That means that richer countries have had to pay higher amounts into the IMF. Now that some of the world's wealthiest countries are struggling economically, that could spell real problems for the IMF. Its donors may not be able to make their payments.

TROUBLE BREWING?

Another potential issue is how the IMF is run. At present, the richest countries have the biggest say in how decisions are made. That means that the United States wields the most power. However, some experts think that the United States will soon be overtaken by China, India and Brazil in economic power.

New economic powers such as China might have different views about how the IMF should do business, and which countries it should lend money to. This change in world power could mean danger for the world economy.

Jobs and Growth: Supporting the European Recovery

Growth is finally picking up in the euro... ...early 20 million people are sti...

In the event of an economic crisis, like that experienced recently by the EU, countries look to the IMF for help.

ask the experts

SOME EXPERTS HAVE CRITICISED THE IMF. SOME HAVE ACCUSED IT OF FAVOURING WEALTHY NATIONS, WHILE OTHERS SAY THAT IT CAN CAUSE MORE PROBLEMS THAN IT SOLVES. MANY EXPERTS THINK THAT ARGENTINA'S HUGE MONTHLY LOAN REPAYMENTS TO THE IMF CAUSED THE COUNTRY TO RUN OUT OF MONEY IN 2001. COULD EXACTLY THE SAME SITUATION HAPPEN ELSEWHERE?

'While many hackers have the knowledge, skills and tools to attack computer systems, they generally lack the motivation to cause severe economic harm.'
Dorothy Denning, Professor of Defence Analysis at the Naval Postgraduate School

We now pay for most things using our phones or computers, which can increase the risk of our money being stolen by computer hackers.

THE DIGITAL ECONOMY

In times gone by, all banking and trade was done with 'real money'. Coins, banknotes and cheques (written notes used to tell banks to pay an amount from one person to another) were exchanged. Now, almost all trade and banking is carried out on computers. Some experts think that this could lead to the downfall of the world economy.

BIG WEAKNESS

Our reliance on using computers to keep track of money could be our greatest weakness. It leaves us open to attack by gangs of computer hackers, experts in computer systems who want to steal vast sums of money. Experts call these people 'cybercriminals'. A few isolated attacks are not enough to damage the economy severely. However, if hackers organised one huge, global attack, it could mean disaster.

CYBERATTACKS

Governments around the world are worried about the possibility of a devastating attack by cybercriminals. They are spending huge amounts of money trying to make their computer systems safe against hacking attacks. This is because if cybercriminals broke into their computer systems, they could steal billions of pounds in seconds.

ENEMY ACTION

Some governments think that spies from other countries are trying to hack into their computers to steal money. They call this 'economic espionage'. If a country succeeded in weakening another's economy using hacking, it would give it a huge advantage. Hacking could be more effective than war in destroying an enemy country.

Many now question the safety of our banking systems. Could technology turn out to be our greatest enemy?

ask the experts

MANY EXPERTS SAY THAT ATTACKS FROM CYBERCRIMINALS AND ENEMY SPIES ARE A HUGE THREAT TO OUR ECONOMY. IN 2011, THE BRITISH GOVERNMENT SAID THAT IT HAD FENDED OFF CYBERATTACKS AGAINST ITS COMPUTER SYSTEMS FROM CHINA AND NORTH KOREA. US GOVERNMENT REPRESENTATIVES SAY THAT THEIR COMPUTER SYSTEMS HAVE ALSO BEEN ATTACKED BY HACKERS.

Some people think that capitalism is a flawed economic system. They say that we would be better off if the government controlled our banks.

" THE
DEBATE

The arguments between capitalists and socialists continue to shape the world we live in. Socialists still believe that isolationism will fix their economy, and make things better for the poor. However, capitalists argue that restricting free trade around the world will harm the economy and make things worse.

THE POLITICS OF MONEY

The economy has always been at the heart of politics. Over the last 100 years, the conflicts between politicians with different opinions on how a country's economy should be run has determined how much money is in our pockets, how we live our lives and even our future.

CAPITALISM AND SOCIALISM

Many countries in the world base their economy on the principles of what is known as capitalism. That broadly means allowing free trade between people and nations. The economy is driven by the supply of, and demand for, goods and services. Some countries around the world reject this idea in favour of an idea called socialism. This aims to distribute money more equally amongst everyone in society. The distribution of wealth is controlled centrally by the country's government.

The recent economic crisis has caused some people to turn towards socialist policies and protest against capitalism.

RISE OF THE ISOLATIONISTS

When the economy crashes and times are hard, it increases the likelihood that countries will turn to 'isolationism'. This is when a country restricts the amount of goods it allows to be bought in, or imported, from elsewhere in the world. Instead of buying goods from other countries, a country promotes the buying of products made at home. This ensures that the money people spend does not leave the country and stays within its economy.

A CHANGING WORLD

Isolationism and socialism are more likely to appeal to people in times of hardship, because they think these policies will improve their lives. They are less likely to consider the wider question of the health of the world economy. Experts warn that if economies around the world experience further turbulance, we could see a rise in isolationism.

FACE FACTS

'Economic isolationism is the wrong way to go. Vibrant, successful growing economies that advance the interests of their citizens engage the global economy.'
John W. Snow, US Secretary of the Treasury, 2003–2006

43

The world economy is always changing. Every day, our economic prospects change as the world's governments and money markets react to the latest news from home and abroad. Economists change their predictions almost as quickly as they change their clothes. So, what do you think will happen in the future?

You're the expert

China has had a recent economic boom, but do you believe its future growth is guaranteed?

FACE FACTS

'Economists have no idea what will happen next year. Well, okay, not no idea. But pretty much no idea.' Henry Blodget, business journalist

BIG QUESTIONS

So what do you think will happen to the world economy in coming years? Will the United States, as some predict, be overtaken by China or India as the world's leading economic superpower? If so, what will this mean for Western countries in years to come? Perhaps you believe that Western countries will find a way to restore and stabilise their positions in the economic world order.

WILL DEBT DESTROY US?

What do you think we should do about the problem of sovereign debt – the money owed by countries to the IMF and others? Will the weight of debt bring down many European countries, or will they find ways to pay it off and guarantee the survival of the eurozone?

FINDING THE ANSWERS

Your answers will not change the world, but they may help you understand the complicated and often confusing world of economics. Different experts have different views about how best to deal with our economic crisis. If you were the expert, what would you decide?

ask the experts

ECONOMISTS TRY TO PREDICT THE FUTURE SO THAT GOVERNMENTS AND BUSINESSES CAN PLAN AHEAD. HOWEVER, VERY FEW GET THEIR PREDICTIONS RIGHT. THIS IS BECAUSE THE ECONOMY IS VERY COMPLICATED AND CAN CHANGE IN A FEW HOURS, DAYS OR WEEKS. ECONOMISTS MAKE A CALCULATED GUESS BASED ON FACTS, BUT IT IS ALWAYS JUST A GUESS.

When it comes to money and economics, nobody can say for sure what will happen in the future.

Glossary

austerity strict government policies in times of economic difficulty, for example cuts to spending on public services and higher taxes

bankrupt legally unable to pay off your debts due to lack of money

capitalism an economic system where trade is controlled by private owners, and not by the government

catastrophic very bad

crisis a bad situation caused by a big event, for example a war or an economic collapse

currency the type of money used by a country, or group of countries, for example the pound and the euro

debt something owed by one person or country to another

economics the study of economies

economist an expert in the study of economics

economy the flow of money in a system, based on the trading of goods and services

employed in work

European Union (EU) a political and economic union of 27 of the countries in Europe

eurozone a group of 17 countries in Europe that all use the euro as their currency

finance money

financial services banking and other industries that specialise in lending money

interest a charge added on to a loan by the lender, in addition to the sum borrowed

International Monetary Fund (IMF) an organisation that lends money to governments, and is funded by 200 countries around the world

isolationism the economic and political idea that a country is better off if it takes care of itself and does not engage with the rest of the world

loan an amount of money given to someone, which they agree to pay back over a period of time

recession a period of time when a country's economy shrinks, instead of growing

repayments money paid to reduce or pay off a debt

socialism an economic system where the resources of a country are managed and distributed by the government, so that wealth is more equally shared between people

sovereign debt money owed by a country's government

stock exchange a place where large quantities of money, goods and shares in companies are bought and sold, for example Wall Street in New York

superpower a country with great wealth and power in the world, for example the United States or China

tax money paid to the government by individuals or organisations

toxic poisonous

trade the buying and selling of things, such as products and services

Books

Booms, Bubbles, & Busts: The Economic Cycle
(The Global Marketplace), Barbara Hollander, Raintree

Global Financial Crisis (Behind the News),
Philip Steele, Wayland

Money and Government (Understanding Money),
Nick Hunter, Raintree

For more information

Websites

There is a useful extended glossary of economic terms
at the Scholastic website:
www.scholastic.com/browse/article.jsp?id=3750579

Find a lot of information on personal finance and economics at:
www.moneymakesense.co.uk

The US Treasury has a great website for kids, full of
information and games on economics, at:
www.treasurydirect.gov/kids/kids.htm

Note to parents and teachers
Every effort has been made by the Publisher to ensure that these websites contain
no inappropriate or offensive material. However, because of the nature of the
Internet, it is impossible to guarantee that the contents of these sites will not be
altered. We strongly advise that Internet access is supervised by a responsible adult.

Index